What Can a Giant Do?

by Mary Louise Cuneo
pictures by Benrei Huang

HarperCollins*Publishers*

Also by Mary Louise Cuneo

How to Grow a Picket Fence

Anne Is Elegant

What Can a Giant Do?
Text copyright © 1994 by Mary Louise Cuneo
Illustrations copyright © 1994 by Benrei Huang
Printed in the U.S.A. All rights reserved.
1 2 3 4 5 6 7 8 9 10
❖
First Edition

Library of Congress Cataloging-in-Publication Data
Cuneo, Mary Louise.
  What can a giant do? / by Mary Louise Cuneo; pictures by Benrei Huang.
    p.   cm.
  Summary: A child relieves his anxiety about being small by imagining a
day spent with a giant.
  ISBN 0-06-021214-4. — ISBN 0-06-021217-9 (lib. bdg.)
  [1. Giants—Fiction. 2. Size—Fiction. 3. Stories in rhyme.]
I. Huang, Benrei, ill. II. Title.
PZ8.3.C916Wh 1994   92-8307
[E]—dc20   CIP
                                                    AC

Because we once—together—seriously delighted in giants, this book is for
Mary Rose, Peter, Martina, Anthony, Michael, and Richard. —M.L.C.

To Shida, my giant —B.H.

What can a giant do?
Peek into your second-floor window
and whisper, "Good morning to you."
Straighten the nest of a robin while
you're getting dressed.

Start out with his giant stride while you
ride in the breezy band of his hat.
Sing a song that could tickle the sky—
a yellow balloon of a song in the blue.

See seven o'clock on a faraway steeple.
Hear the small seven strikings and count
them for you.

What can a giant do?
Step over a river and its shadowy
   blinking turtles and fish.
Blow on an acre of dandelion puffs,
   and make an acre-sized wish.

What can a giant do?
Wish for a secret mountain and climb
  to the top with you.
Hold on to his hat in the tip-top wind.

Point to the ocean. Wave to the little
ships waving, some of them pinned
to the edge.

Turn to the prairie. "Look! White sailing
houses are ships on this sea!"

Turn to the town. There's a little
parade down one of its streets,
with the soft summer flutter of
everyone there.

What can a giant do!
Everyone there but you—
    you, feeling bad, looking ready to cry.
Far, far away, the parade going by.

What can a giant do?
Borrow a cloud and ride on the cloud
   with you.
A long shining elephant ride in the sky.
Around and around the mountaintop.
A cheering-up elephant ride in the sky.

What can a giant do?
Return the cloud when the cloud is tired.
Stretch out for a rest round the mountain
with you.

What can a giant do?
Feel the moon telling time in a moon-
    colored sky.
Open his eyes, and smile at the moon.
Stand up on his mountain and whisper,
    "Good-bye."

What can a giant do?
Tiptoe down his mountain with you.
Over its trees.
Over the dandelion acre for wishes.
Over the river, its turtles and fishes.

Past the street remembering fluttery
people.
Past the faraway clock on its silent
steeple.

What can a giant do?
Find the robin's nest,
  and your bed
  and your dream for you.

Peek into your sleeping window at last
and whisper, "Now, that's what a giant
can do."